BY ETHEL AND LEONARD KESSLER

Slush Slush!

Parents' Magazine Press

New York

For Mrs. Arlene Clinkscale
and all the children at Summit Park School
who love those snowy days

Library of Congress Cataloging in Publication Data

Kessler, Ethel.
   Slush, slush!
   SUMMARY: A youngster explores some things that can
be done in snow—sledding, throwing snowballs, building
snowmen, and more.
   [1. Snow—Fiction. 2. Stories in rhyme]
I. Kessler, Leonard P.,   joint author.
II. Title.
PZ7.K483Sl   [E]   73-4445
ISBN 0-8193-0675-4   ISBN 0-8193-0676-2 (lib. bdg.)

Snow sky,

Snowflakes.

Snow.
Snow.
Snow.

S is for
Snow!
Slush, slush.

S is for snowflake,
cold and wet.
It falls on my nose
and just on the tip
of my tongue.

Here I go
making tracks
in the clean, fresh snow.

Slush, slush!

Look!
Who has been here?

A cat?
A dog?
A rabbit?
A bird?

Someone else has
been here too.
I know who.
I think it is. . .

YOU!

With a stick
I can make a letter in the snow.
Can you guess?
Yes.
I can make an S.

S is for sledding
down a slippery hill.
Look out.
Look out below.
S is for snow.

Sparrows are searching
for something to eat.
They can't find food
on a snow covered street.
Here birds.
Here birds.
Here's food for you to eat.

Silly snowman
round and fat,
with a carrot nose
and daddy's old hat.
I'll toss a snowball
at that hat.
Plop!

S is for the sun
that melts the
snowman,
and melts the
snowballs,
and melts the snow
that turns to gray
slush.

Slush, slush.

It's time
to get these cold wet boots
off my frozen feet.
It's time to go home.
It's time to eat.

It's time for
soup!
Soup's just right,
hot soup for supper
on a snowy night.

Night sky.
Howling winds.
Blowing snow.
Swirling snow
up against my window.

Snow.

Snow.

Snow.

S is for snowstorm.

Snowy night.
Snowflakes fly.
Polka dots
in the cold,
dark sky.

Snowy night.
Stormy night.
Turn off the light.
Good night.